What You Do Is Easy, What I Do Is Hard

BY **JAKE WOLF**

PICTURES BY **ANNA DEWDNEY**

Greenwillow Books New York

Watercolors, gouache paints, colored pencils, and a black pen were used
for the full-color art. The text type is Esprit Book.
Text copyright © 1996 by Jake Wolf
Illustrations copyright © 1996 by Anna Dewdney
All rights reserved. No part of this book may be reproduced or
utilized in any form or by any means, electronic or mechanical,
including photocopying, recording, or by any information storage
and retrieval system, without permission in writing from the Publisher,
Greenwillow Books, a division of William Morrow & Company, Inc.,
1350 Avenue of the Americas, New York, NY 10019.
Printed in Hong Kong by South China Printing Company (1988) Ltd.
First Edition   10   9   8   7   6   5   4   3   2   1

Library of Congress Cataloging-in-Publication Data
Wolf, Jake.
What you do is easy, what I do is hard / by Jake Wolf ;
pictures by Anna Dewdney.
      p.   cm.
Summary: Convinced that what he does all day long is much
more difficult than tasks performed by others, a squirrel takes
over the activities of a bee, an ant, a robin, and a spider.
ISBN 0-688-13440-8
[1. Squirrels—Fiction.   2. Work—Fiction.]   I. Title.
PZ7.W818552Wh   1996   [E]—dc20
95-5467   CIP   AC

What You Do Is Easy, What I Do Is Hard

BY JAKE WOLF
PICTURES BY ANNA DEWDNEY

Greenwillow Books   New York

Library of Congress Cataloging-in-Publication Data
Wolf, Jake.
What you do is easy, what I do is hard / by Jake Wolf ;
pictures by Anna Dewdney.
       p.   cm.
Summary: Convinced that what he does all day long is much
more difficult than tasks performed by others, a squirrel takes
over the activities of a bee, an ant, a robin, and a spider.
ISBN 0-688-13440-8
[1. Squirrels—Fiction.   2. Work—Fiction.]   I. Title.
PZ7.W818552Wh   1996   [E]—dc20
95-5467   CIP   AC

For Betsy,
who makes everything a little easier
—A. D.

It was late afternoon on a hot day in May.
The bee came buzzing under the dogwood tree
and landed on the grass.

"I'm so tired!" said the bee. "All day long I've been
flying from one apple blossom to another, gathering
pollen."

"What you do is easy," said the squirrel, from a
branch above. "What I do is hard."

"Oh, really?" said the bee.

"Yes, sir," said the squirrel. "I go running up and
down tall trees from dawn to dusk, looking for nuts."

The ant came staggering through the grass and settled down in the shade.

"I'm a wreck," he said. "Been crawling in and out of people's kitchens since morning, searching for crumbs. When I'm lucky enough to find one, I have to carry the huge thing home on my back."

"What you do is easy," said the squirrel. "What I do is hard. Try building a nest at the top of a tree in a high wind."

The robin landed on the branch next to the squirrel. "Nest, you say? I've built plenty. They're just a bunch of twigs. Try digging for earthworms in the hard ground for a few hours. You bust your beak."

"What you do is easy," said the squirrel. "I leap from one tree to another, high above the ground. That's hard."

The spider came down the trunk of the dogwood
tree and collapsed on the grass.

"I've never been this pooped," she said. "Five days
on the same web."

"What you do is easy," said the squirrel.

"I'd like to see you spin a giant, perfect web," said
the spider, "while you're dangling upside down."

"I could do it," said the squirrel, "if I had the
materials."

"Well, go find some," said the spider. "Stop talking
and start spinning."

"While you're at it," said the bee, "let's see you
   collect some pollen."
"And dig some earthworms," said the robin.
"And gather some crumbs, too," said the ant,
"if it's so easy!"
   They all stared at the squirrel.
"You think I can't do all those easy things?" said
   the squirrel. "I'll show you!" He marched away.

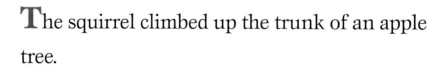

The squirrel climbed up the trunk of an apple
tree.

"Now where are those apple blossoms with all
the pollen?" he said.

The nearest cluster was on a long, thin branch.

The squirrel crawled out on the branch.

"I do this kind of thing every day," he said.

"This is a cinch."

The branch began to tremble and bend.

"Oh-oh," said the squirrel.

He tried to hang on. The branch bent even more, until it was pointing at the ground.

The squirrel went sliding headfirst, taking all the apple blossoms with him. He hit the ground with a thud. The branch snapped back. Pollen came down on his head like snow.

"Ka-choo!" sneezed the squirrel. "Ka-choo!"

"I'll start the crumb-gathering now," he said.

"That will give me a chance to catch my breath."

The squirrel walked through backyards until he saw a house that might have crumbs in its kitchen. He peered through the screen door. He could see pots piled in the sink.

"Excellent," he said.

He opened the screen door and stepped into the kitchen. There were plenty of crumbs.

"I knew this would be easy," he said.

The screen door swung shut on his tail. The squirrel let out a shriek.

He was pulling his tail free when he heard
growling. It was coming from the next room.
A moment later a big brown dog came charging
into the kitchen, barking.

The squirrel raced out the door. He jumped up
onto a fence, then into a tree, and didn't stop
climbing until he was high in the branches,
hidden by the leaves.

"That was a close call," he said. "I believe I'll
rest for a while, and just watch for earthworms."

There didn't seem to be any earthworms.
The squirrel went to the next tree, and then
to another one. At last he saw an earthworm
wriggling partway out of the dirt.

The squirrel jumped to the ground. "Excuse
me," he said. "Are you coming or going?"

"Does it matter to you?" said the earthworm.

"I just need to borrow an earthworm for a little
while," said the squirrel.

"For what?" said the earthworm.

"To show a robin how easy it is to get one," said
the squirrel. "Would you mind?"

"Mind?" said the earthworm. "Mind? That's all
I need—to get handed over to some hungry
robin."

The earthworm squirmed into the dirt and
disappeared.

The squirrel decided to start building the spider web.
"How hard could it be?" he said.

He remembered where a blue-and-white kite
was stuck in a tree. The kite had lots of string.
"I'll make a web out of kite string," said the
squirrel. "This will be a piece of cake."

A few minutes later the squirrel was looping
kite string through the branches of an oak tree,
stretching it to a nearby maple and back again.
He began zigzagging string back and forth
between the trees.

The squirrel stood on a branch, admiring his web.
It looked a little bit like a hammock and a little bit
like a basketball net.
The squirrel stepped back and fell off the branch.
He landed in the web. His foot snagged in the strings
and he dangled, bouncing upside down.
"Upside down is not so easy," he said to himself.

There was a loud growl. The big brown dog was glaring at him.

"Stay out of other people's kitchens," said the dog. She gave the squirrel a shove with one paw. The squirrel went spinning around like the propeller on a toy airplane.

The brown dog left, but the squirrel went around and around until the strings were twisted as tight as they could go. There was a pause.

Then the squirrel began to spin in the other direction, faster and faster, until his foot broke loose and he fell to the ground.

The bee, the ant, the spider, and the robin were
waiting at the dogwood tree when the squirrel
came back, walking slowly.

"So where's all the pollen?" said the bee.

"Where are the crumbs?" said the ant.

"Where's the perfect web?" said the spider.

"I don't see any earthworms," said the robin.

"I ran into problems," said the squirrel.

"Problems?" said the bee. "Like what?"

"Pollen problems," said the squirrel.

"What about crumb-gathering?" said the ant.

"I had crumb-gathering problems, too," said
 the squirrel.

"Any web problems?" said the spider.

"Webs are not easy," said the squirrel.

"Earthworms?" said the robin.

"Leave me alone," said the squirrel.
 He looked at the ground.

"It was all too hard. Everything."

"Well," said the robin after a moment, "we'd
  have a very hard time doing what squirrels do."
"That's the truth," said the spider.
"What we do is hard," said the ant, "and what
  you do is hard."

"Would anybody care for a walnut or an acorn?"
said the squirrel. "I have a nice selection."

"A snack would be nice," said the ant.

"I could go for that," said the spider.

"Me, too," said the bee. "Would anyone like some
honey?"

"Honey and walnuts—*mmm*," said the robin.

"I'd like some, too," said the squirrel. "It's been
a long day."